BROKEN

Not

BITTER

BY: ANGELINA WILSON

Publishers address:

Niagara Falls, NY. 14305

Email:Mrs.author@myself.com

Facebook.com/Authroess Angelina Wilson

Instagram.com/mrs._author2019

DEDICATION

This book is dedicated to my mother, Yvonne Johnson. Thank you for always being a mother first. I love you, mom.

To the bitter baby moms, bitter ex's, and bitter ex-wives, I hope you all find it in you to heal accordingly.

To any woman who has overcome BROKENESS, this one is also for you Queens.

Broken- (of a person) having given up all hope; despairing.

Bitter-(of people or their feelings or behavior) angry, hurt, or resentful because of one's bad experiences or a sense of unjust treatment.

TABLE OF CONTENTS

PROLOGUE
Summer of 1998

*I*f the temperature outside was as hot as the temperature inside of my home, I knew it was going to be a hot summer. My parents were in a heated argument, something I was all too familiar with.

"When you have a husband, you must submit to him. Why is that so hard for you to do Elora? You heard what the pastor said." My father was the true definition of a hypocrite, and my mother allowed it because she was too submissive. I sat in my room listening to my parents bicker back and forth, taking in all of their toxic energy.

My father, Carlon Henderson made sure we were in church faithfully every Sunday. It wasn't that he loved the sermons, or that he paid his tithes every week, it was the exact opposite of all that. He needed the word of God to use as a tool against my mother, to make her feel guilty so that she would never leave.

Being in a broken home, I picked up on a lot of what was going on around me. At the age of ten, I already knew my daddy committed adultery way too many times. I also knew that my mother continued to turn the other cheek until the problems were directly in her face and turning the cheek was no longer an option.

"Submit to a Godly man Carlon, that's what God was talking about in the Bible. How can I submit to a man who is a cheating backstabber, and is having a child out of wedlock? A man who has committed adultery on multiple occasions, a man who sits in the house of the lord and pretends to be the holiest saint." My mother's voice rumbled throughout the house like a stampede, her voice trembling with rage.

I could taste the salty tears falling from my eyes. I knew our home which seemed so perfect from the outside, was slowly deteriorating. I couldn't believe my dad was having a baby, and the baby wasn't by my mom. Where would this leave me? Would my daddy still want me? Or would he leave like so many of my peers' fathers? I thought.

I had some questions, but I didn't want to interrupt. One thing my parents didn't play about, was kids in grown folk's business.

"If you spare the rod, you'll spoil the child," was the most quoted scripture in this house and my dad didn't spare the rod at all.

"God says we must forgive. When you took your vows, you took those vows before God."

"So did you." My mother spoke up.

"But I'm not the one who is trying to get a divorce, you are. My dad's voice started to grow angry, he always did that as a form of intimidation.

"I'm not the one who cheated, you did." My mother responded. Her tone was a lot calmer now, I was hoping she wasn't giving into his bullshit. One thing about my mom, she was old skool. Even if she was hurting or even dying inside, she refused to have a one-parent household. The sad part about it was, a blind man could see that she wasn't happy. I didn't want my mom to stay because of me, I wanted her to leave because of me. I wanted her to take us and find us our own home, that way I could see her smile again. It's been so long since I saw my mother smile, I was starting to wonder if my dad knocked her teeth out. He was always physically abusive, I didn't put anything past him. I didn't want my mom making any more excuses to stay, she deserved to be happy, and I did too.

"Listen, Elora. If it makes you feel any better the affair happened nine years ago. I didn't know about any of this until yesterday. That one time we separated all those years ago I made a mistake, but we were on a break." My dad was pleading now, but I didn't hear my mom say anything.

"Her mother reached out to me and she needs help. I have to let our daughter stay with us."

"Our daughter?" My mom's voice reached an octave I never heard before, she didn't even sound the same as her voice roared like a lioness.

"Bang! Bang!"

I heard a few bangs, then a loud thud. I was too scared to come out of my room, it wasn't until my mom opened the door that I knew it was my dad, who must have taken the blow this time.

"Let's go Carlonna. NOW!" My mom shouted at me, which she never does. I jumped off my bed and did as I was told, but I grabbed some things to put in my bookbag.

"Where's dad?" I questioned.

My mom just ignored me and headed for the front door, I followed right in her footsteps. I wanted to know if my dad was alright, even though he was a bad man he was still my father. We headed for our minivan, I hopped in the backseat and buckled up. My mom pulled off in silence, I looked at her distorted face in the rearview mirror. Her face was damp, so I knew she had been crying. She had on sunglasses, trying to hide what I already knew. Her hair was messy, but it didn't hide the fact that she was still perfectly imperfect. Her caramelized skin was always glowing and giving off a radiant vibe, even the sun rays had to be jealous at how her skin shined so effortlessly. When she kept her hair done it reached past her behind. She didn't have a butt, her tiny figure would give supermodels a run for their money though. One thing I got from my mom was good hair.

I sat back in the backseat and enjoyed the ride, it wasn't often that I saw the daylight, dad was very strict.

Days turned into a few more days at Grandma Elane's house. We ended up crashing at my mom; mother's house. In those few days I felt better than I ever have, I enjoyed playing with my cousins and getting to know relatives that my dad always forbade me to see. "You shouldn't associate yourself with the likes of devils," was his response anytime I asked to visit my relatives.

All of the laughs, good food, and catching up came to an abrupt end, on the fifth day of us being at Grandmas. I knew my dad had been calling my mom a lot, but I didn't think she'd be a coward and run back so soon.

Once we pulled into the driveway of our five bedrooms wanna be perfect home, my dad quickly opened the front door. The first thing I noticed was a huge bandage on the side of his forehead, which I knew was from their fight. Mom got out first and he grabbed her bags, I carried my own of course. I didn't have a great relationship with my dad, due to the brokenness in the household. Instead of loving me, he showered me with expensive gifts in hopes it would fix our disconnected relationship.

"Come inside." My dad was smiling from ear to ear, as he hurried us along.

Once inside my jaw dropped almost instantly.

My dad walked past us, to stand in front of us.

"Welcome Carlise to the family." He said happily like we were supposed to welcome her with open arms. To my surprise, my mom walked up to her and greeted her with a hug, like she was her long lost daughter. I just kept glancing at her, we had similar features and the same mocha-colored skin as our father. Her round face and perky lips, matched mine perfectly, only she had a Marilyn Monroe mole on her face. Her oval-shaped light brown eyes were identical to mine, only my eyebrows were perfectly arched, hers were thick and unplucked. It also didn't make it any better she was named after my dad, just as I was.

Why did women do that dumb shit, daddy name Carlon, let's name the daughter Carlonna? Like everybody knows who my daddy is, why make it more obvious and give me this wack ass name. I thought to myself. I was trying to take in all of this foolishness, I still couldn't take my eyes off Carlise. She was the spitting image of myself and my dad, there was no denying that this little bitch was my father's child.

CHAPTER 1
New Edition

I was forced to become a big sister to someone I didn't know, according to my dad I was the oldest, so it was my responsibility to form a bond. I felt like I was paying for my dad's mistakes and I wasn't happy about it. He needed to be in here trying to be a dad, instead of forcing me to be a sister. Carlise wasn't bad at all though, to be honest, she kept to herself, but it was her presence that bothered me. I went from being the only child to having another kid move right into our home, invading my privacy. I was livid.

"Hey Carlonna, you want to color with me?" Carlise was very soft-spoken, she looked at me gleefully anticipating my answer.

"No!" Was all that I could give her. No explanation, no remorse, just a blunt, and formal NO. The look in Carlise's eyes told me her feelings were hurt, but who was I to show any sympathy. She didn't show any sympathy when she just came waltzing into our lives, destroying our home. I left her in the playroom and walked out, I didn't have the patients to be around her.

"Hey honey, how are things going with your sister?" My dad asked as he walked down the hall towards me. I gave him a blank stare and turned away, making my way to my room.

"Keep this up Lonna, you won't have a birthday party." My dad retorted.

I closed my room door and laid in bed, the last thing on my mind was a party. I always loved the big parties my dad threw for me, but if it included Carlise, I wanted no parts of it.

A light knock tapped my room door as I laid under my canopy, staring out the window. I didn't acknowledge whoever was knocking, and for Carlise's sake it better not have been her.

"Hey, Lonna." My mother whispered like she wasn't supposed to be in my room or something.

"Hey," I replied dryly letting her know I wasn't in the mood.

"Listen, Lonna. I know these sudden changes are not something that you will adapt to overnight, but you're just going to have to deal with it."

"So you dealt with it that fast. Just let dad cheat, then come crawling back like a lost ant looking for a piece of bread?" I didn't mean to say that, but for some reason, my smart ass mouth wouldn't stay shut.

My mom was on my ass before I could blink, her chest heaved up and down like she was trying to catch her breath but couldn't. Her eyes narrowed into slits, she clenched her fist to refrain from hitting me.

"As bad as I want to smack your ass into next year, I'm going to pause real quick. The last thing I need is a CPS case, from beating the hell out of my daughter. Your mouth is reckless and before I walk out of here, I'm going to school you real quick." My mom calmed down and finally got her breathing under control, she kept her eyes fixed on me while sitting on my pink furry chaise, that matched my pink furry rug. I sat quietly because I knew my mom was upset, she never turned into Cruella De Vil in a blink of an eye like that before.

"First of all little girl, lost is something I've never been nor will I ever be, so let's get that straight." I continued to listen to my mom while acknowledging every word she said.

"I know you see what goes on in this house and I'm sorry that you have to witness the arguments and fights, but you have somewhere to lay your big head at. You have food to put in your smart ass mouth and clothes to put on your back, you have a cell phone, a huge bed, and other things most children can't afford to have."

I knew my mom was speaking the truth, but none of that was the point. She was making this about me when it was about that bastard child in the other room.

"Look at me, Lonna." My mom continued her lecture.

"A man will only do what you allow, he will try to skate around you in circles until you're dizzy and lose all your common sense, but only if you allow him. I have allowed so much that I forgot my worth, but I'm making it so that you know yours. If I have to sacrifice my soul for you, to make sure you're set for life and financially stable, then you can bet your daddy's black ass I will. I'm not happy Lonna, but I'm comfortable. You may think I'm stupid, but that's far from the truth. No one can run game on me, baby girl because I already know the game." "And just so you know, I knew about Carlise before your daddy even told me, so don't ever think your mama is a fool. Now if you don't remember anything from this conversation remember this, nothing gets past a woman who's on her shit."

I just smiled at my mom, her confidence overshadowed any doubts that I had, and I knew I could trust her wisdom. My mom reached down and kissed me on my cheeks as she rubbed the top of my head. She looked at me seriously before whispering.

"Lonna, don't you ever compare me to no damn ant. I'm a bad bitch, don't forget that." My mom started laughing, which made me join her. That was the first time in a while we shared a laugh, and she was actually smiling. After our embrace, my mom headed out, but not before stopping at my bedroom door.

"You may want to get used to your sister being around, she'll be staying with us longer than we anticipated." My mother didn't give me any explanation before closing my door behind her. I guess the whole couple months thing was all a lie, my dad probably already knew she'd be living with us forever and I wasn't the least bit excited about it. I guess I had to take heed to my mother's advice, but I refused to just be comfortable, that wasn't something I was going to accept. Since I didn't have a choice now, I promised that I would have choices when I got older. For now, I had to welcome the new edition to our family. I had to face the reality that, my little sister was here to stay.

CHAPTER 2

Comfortable

*I*f I must say so myself, giving Carlise a chance may have been a good thing. I had to understand that she was a victim in this situation just as much as I was, and for that, I had to sympathize with her also. She's been here for over five months now, so did I really have a choice?

A few days ago we learned that Carlise's mother died, she was in a car accident and didn't make it. Carlise wouldn't come out of her room, and I felt bad for her. I couldn't imagine life without my mother, so I could only imagine what she was going through.

I knocked on Carlise's door lightly, hoping she wouldn't reject me.

"Come in." I heard a soft whimper and entered the room. Carlise's newly furnished room was in shambles, everything was thrown all over the place. Her posters of Chris Brown were ripped which was surprising since she was head over heels with him. Her furry rug was cut up and her bed was broken, the mirror that hung from her wall was shattered. I looked at Carlise in dismay, she stood in front of me with her hand soaking in blood.

Carlise's face was soaked with tears, her long black hair was knotted and her eyes were now red and puffy. Light whimpers escaped her mouth, but nothing came out. It sounded like she wanted to talk but she couldn't get the words out. I never in a million years thought I'd be in this situation, but here I was. I grabbed a ripped shirt from off the floor and wrapped it around her hand, I tied it tight enough to slow the bleeding down.

"Why my mommy Carlonna. Wwhhyy...?" Carlise cried out in such agony that it tugged at my heart, that hurt came from deep down inside of her. All I could do was hug her, she was only nine and already lost the most important person in her life. I held her in my arms and cried with her, I didn't have an answer but I did have a shoulder and I didn't mind her crying on it.

A knock on the door caused us to direct our attention towards it, our father poked his head in.

"Everything alright in here with my girls?"

"How can you possibly ask that question?" Carlise spoke. "Just because you didn't care about my momma doesn't mean she didn't have people who loved her. I'm ashamed to be your daughter, I don't even know you. The only parent I knew is dead now," Carlise shouted as my dad looked at her in shock. His face went from pleasant to vexed. Carlise tensed in my arms as she sensed she struck a nerve, in all reality, she was telling the truth.

"What's going on up here?" My mom eased into the room, she must have heard all the commotion from downstairs.

"There is nothing left to be said here," our dad replied calmly as he walked out of the room, leaving Carlise wondering if she took things too far.

My mom walked over and consoled Carlise and me.

"I'm so sorry honey, your mom and I at least got to put our differences aside and be women about the situation. If it makes you feel any better, we promised each other to always look out for you girls. I promised her that if anything happened to her I'd look after you, and vice versa. I'm not your biological mom and God knows I'd never want to take her place, but just know you have a mother figure in me, and I promise to love you like my own." My mother's words touched me, as Carlise balled her eyes out. I knew if I felt it, she did too. I gained a new level of respect for my mom, she was so selfless and for that, I would always have the utmost respect for her.

"Come down to the bathroom, so I can clean your hand." My mom concluded after the three of us embraced.

I think I grew attached to Carlise quickly because I saw myself, even though our dad was in the household, he wasn't necessarily a father. It was so much I needed to tell Carlise and I knew eventually we would have that conversation, right now I had to push my feelings aside and get comfortable in an uncomfortable situation.

CHAPTER 3
Sister Sister

T he relationship between Carlise and I grew over the last six years, we were always together like peanut butter and jelly. If I went left she went left, if I skipped school, she would too. We were both smart and were on the honors committee, so skipping class a few times out the year wouldn't hurt.

"Hey sis, the football team is having a party tonight, you want to go?" Carlise asked excitedly, as she walked up to my locker.

"Now you know daddy ain't having that," I told her.

"That's why we have to sneak out, come on Carlonna it will be fun." Carlise was pressing the issue while adding her little charm that I couldn't say no to.

"If we get busted you owe me," I said, knowing I would regret this. Carlise hugged me before walking off to her locker, her friend Ghani followed closely behind her. If I didn't know any better, I would have sworn Ghani was into my sister. Carlise never gave any indication that she was into girls, but those two were always so secretive around each other.

I knew if our dad found out we weren't home and snuck out to a party, we would be in a world of trouble. If it wasn't about the church, singing in the choir, or praying, he didn't want to hear anything about it. The only time we were able to breathe was when he was out of town on his business trips, and we took full advantage of that shit. My mom was always busy writing her songs, she found love in music. I guess since my dad couldn't love her the right way, she had to find something to fill that void.

We had a recording studio in the basement of the house now, and you could find her down there singing her heart out. Over the years my mom continued to endure heartache from our dad, she thought her tears were silent, but they were loud because not only did I hear her cries, I felt them.

After the final bell rang, the halls were cluttered with students. I waited at the dismissal door for Carlise like I always did, moments later she came prancing around the corner with Ghani.

"You ready to head home sis?" Carlise asked as she walked up to me. I nodded my head and we left. Ghani followed us, which confused me.

"Where is she going?" I questioned.

"Damn Lonna, chill. She lives a few blocks from us, so she'll be walking with us."

The rest of the walk was silent, besides the light chuckles that transpired between Carlise and Ghani.

Once we made it past Millennium Park, Carlise gave Ghani a hug and a look that I wasn't familiar with was exchanged between the two.

"Have a great day Carlonna," Ghani said while waving at me. I smeared a fake smile across my face and waved back without saying anything.

"What the hell is your issue with her? She's one of the sweetest girls I know." Carlise ask. It didn't make it any better that she was sticking up for her. I also didn't know what my issue was with Ghani, since I didn't even know her.

"Let me find out big sis is jealous?"

"Girl bye." I laughed while dismissing Carlise's comment.

"Girl can't nobody replace you, were blood sisters. Sister sister, bitch."

I just looked at Carlise and smiled. In all actuality, I wanted to ask her something but I didn't know if she would be offended.

"Why are you looking at me like that? I know when something is on your mind so just spit it out," Carlise said.

"I don't know Lease, maybe I'm just overreacting," I told her, calling her by her nickname.

"Tell me." She whined.

"Okay but don't get mad." I paused and took a deep breath, I didn't want to offend my sister but I also wanted her to be real with me.

"Are you into Ghani?" I blurted out.

"Why do you ask that?" Carlise was too dark for her blushing to be noticeable, but she was for sure blushing with a huge smile on her face.

"Are you standing there blushing?" I asked. While giving her an, "are you fuckin' serious right now" look.

"Oh whatever Lonna, you wouldn't understand." Carlise dismissed me promptly and started walking again.

"My bad Lease, I didn't mean to hurt your feelings, I didn't mean anything by it." I wanted to assure her that I wasn't judging her, I just wasn't expecting her to be into girls. She never came off as a lesbian, bisexual, or whatever she classified herself as. She was my sister and regardless, I was going to love her.

"All of my life I had to hide who I Am. Why should my preferences be a problem for anyone?" She stopped walking momentarily, before looking at me and then continued her rant.

"If anyone should understand, it should be you. We eat, smell, and breathe church. Were in highschool and never partied before unless we snuck out, we never pulled an all-nighter. The only time friends can come over is when school work is involved, so what better way to make an excuse for Ghani to come around? I knew I liked girls since I was eight, and nothing will change my mind now."

"Better not let dad find out." I gave her a knowing look and continued to walk, it was one thing to tell me, but Carlon Henderson was not having that.

I understood my sister completely, but dad wouldn't be too understanding. I could already hear him now.

"What you're doing is an abomination to God, women should not be with women and men should not be with men. If God wanted you to be with a woman then he would have created Adam and Steve, instead of Adam and Eve." That was his favorite line when it came to homosexuality.

I wanted Carlise to know I had her back, so I grabbed her arm and we skipped the rest of the way home. I loved her no matter her sexual orientation, as long as those little whores didn't come before me. However, getting dad to see the bigger picture wasn't going to be easy. One thing those church hypocrites did was make sure they called out everybody's sins besides their own. I knew for sure that this was considered a big sin and if dad ever found out about Carlise, I could only imagine the extreme he would take to punish her.

CHAPTER 4
Leaving the Nest

oday was all about me, I was having a huge grad party and everyone was welcome. Two years flew by like a fast forward button was being pressed, but I wasn't complaining. I was done with school and college was something I'd get into soon, but for now, I was going to enjoy my young life. Carlise still had another year to go and hiding Ghani was causing her to lose focus. She was still maintaining good grades, but her attendance wasn't great like it used to be. Since she couldn't bring Ghani home, she skipped classes to spend time with her. They had this special kind of love and every time I was in their presence I felt it, Carlise was a different person around Ghani. The love they had for each other was obvious,

I didn't know how our parents didn't catch on a long time ago.

I looked over by the pool, the guests were along the side of it enjoying the fresh summer air. I was honored to invite everyone into my childhood home, it was updated but it was still the same. Growing up in Lakeview shielded us from most of Chicago, but what our parents didn't know was we got around. So, when some of the corner boys and teens from the public schools started coming in, my parents looked at me like I was crazy.

"Lonna, you must be out of your mind, inviting these hoodlums into our home." My dad was mumbling in my ear, his stale breath made the back of my hair stand up. He was inches away from me holding my arm, I knew he was pissed.

"Dad, relax. You see their skin, well look at ours. These are our people, whether you like it or not. Just because you took us out of the hood and ran from your history, doesn't mean I'm going to run from mine. Now if you'll excuse me I'm going to enjoy my company." I left my dad standing in the kitchen, I didn't have time for his shit today. He said I could have a party and invite whomever I wanted and that's what I did. This party was open to the public, but I did take precautions. Everyone was checked at the gate, including their cars. I wasn't that stupid.

I made my way over by the outside bar, some fresh air was needed. My dad always had a way of ruining my mood. Carlise and Ghani were inside of the pool splashing each other, they were in a world of their own. Ghani's tiny little body danced around the pool, her two-piece bikini was designed by her. She was an inspiring designer, and her skills spoke through her work. She was a bright skin beauty with chinky golden brown eyes and thick natural lashes. She could pass for Ariana Grande's little sister, there was a striking resemblance between the two.

I grabbed a wine cooler from the bar and sat down alone to have a drink. I was in deep thoughts, taking in everything around me.

"Is someone sitting here beautiful?"

A deep husky voice snapped me out of my daze, I didn't have to look up to know this man was Scrumptious.

"Not at all," I replied without looking up at him.

"You're the birthday girl right?"

"How'd you know?"

"Well, there's about thirty pictures of a girl who looks just like you hanging up. Unless you have an identical twin, then I could understand."

I let out a light giggle, before making eye contact with the most delicious piece of honey glazed ham I ever saw. He looked like a fresh piece of meat, waiting to get chewed up on Thanksgiving day. The guy who sat beside me was beyond fine. He was the color of caramel, with a freshly trimmed goatee and neat cornrows. His swag screamed West Garfield or Englewood. I studied Chicago all of my life because it was important to me to know where I come from. Just because it may have looked like he came from that area, didn't necessarily mean he did. He was dressed like a dope boy, and I could tell he was a little older than I was.

"That was kind of a dumb question," I finally replied after taking in all of his deliciousness. I was still a virgin, so these feelings I felt were getting the best of me. I couldn't describe the pulling I felt in my kitty like my pussy muscles were doing pushups or something. Then my heart felt like it was beating out of my chest, I was nervous.

"So where are you from, and what's your name?" I asked bluntly, trying to sound unbothered while trying to stop the knot from forming in my throat.

"I'm 20, my name is Fazio and I'm from Englewood, born and raised.

"I knew it," I said out loud unknowingly.

"You knew what?" Fazio looked at me waiting for a response, but something else caught my attention.

There was commotion in the front of the house, even with the music blasting I could hear my mother's high-pitched voice. I was hoping it wasn't my guest causing a disturbance, or I would be shutting this shit down. I left Fazio at the bar and made my way back inside the house. When I got close, I heard an unfamiliar voice overpowering my mother's now screechy voice.

"I didn't make him on my own, I ain't raising him on my own." The lady said. I peaked my head around the corner and was shocked to see a younger girl with a kid. She had to be in her late twenties, while my dad was well over fifty.

"You got one leaving, mine as well raise this one." The girl laughed hysterically while placing a bag on the front steps. The little boy looked to be no more than five, he was the spitting image of my dad. He looked more like my dad than me or Carlise. My mom walked away from the door, we made immediate eye contact and she put her head down. Once she started to walk past me, I lifted her chin and kissed her forehead. She headed to her safe place; the basement.

My dad just stood at the door looking stupid. The little boy was crying because his mom took off, he was now standing with a stranger.

"Why are you bringing these hoodlums into our home?" I whispered into my dad's ear. He looked at me perplexed, but surprisingly he stayed quiet. I was disgusted by my dad, he continued to hurt my mom for his selfish reasons. I refused to sit and watch my mom die because she didn't want to leave, if she wasn't going to leave then I was. It was time for me to leave the nest and become my own woman, I had to get away from this shit before it consumed me.

I just shook my head at my dad and walked away. If he wanted more kids, why didn't he just say that?

CHAPTER 5
Out Of The Closet

Carlise was pissed at me when she found out I was moving out. My mother said she knew I would be the first to go, but she would remain. So, there she was in a home raising other people's kids. Little Carlon has been there for two months now, he was five years old and I felt so bad for him. His mom named him right after my dad, he was a Jr. I knew my mom's heart was shattered, but she would never admit it. I found out a few years ago that she couldn't have more kids, that's why I was her only child.

"What's your excuse for staying? I'm gone now you can't blame me," I asked my mom over the phone while lying in my king size bed.

"For better or worse, richer or poorer, in sickness and in health, till death do us part!" My mom whispered into the phone.

"You forgot to love and to cherish." After I said that, I wanted to take it back. My mom's sobs could be heard as she sat quietly on the other end. Not long after, I heard the piano. She started singing so beautifully and all I could do was cry with her. Her voice was so angelic as she sang her favorite church song, "His Eye Is On The Sparrow."

"You alright beautiful?" Fazio's voice startled me, I started wiping my tears. I didn't need him thinking I was a weak bitch, ready to run back home.

"Yeah, I'm good," I assured him, after hanging up with my mom.

"I don't mean to be in your business but, your mom just needs some new dick. Right now your daddy knows he got her trapped, she's been with him so long that they're comfortable living how they do. Now if she goes and finds some new dick, some good dick that will keep her wanting more, she'll get over your daddy. Women have an emotional attachment when sex is involved, especially when they have been fuckin that long. Once she's emotionally attached to a new dick, she will be out here singing Amazing Grace at 2 am."

I just looked at Fazio quizzically, because what did he know? Since we've been involved, he never once dropped jewels like that. Little did he know, I was going to keep everything he said locked in the back of my mind.

After my graduation party, Fazio and I stayed in touch, and as soon as I was ready to move he had a huge truck and workers waiting at my beck and call. Ever since then, we've been rockin' hard.

Fazio didn't necessarily stay with me, but he did contribute to helping me get this apartment. I received $5,000 a month from my dad to cover my bills and necessities, he always used money to bury his guilt but if he was giving I was receiving. I couldn't afford the housing in Lakeview, so I went for the next best affordable place; Bucktown.

When Fazio offered to pay for everything and to place me in a better neighborhood, I declined. I refused to let a man have anything to hold against me, once he starts paying for shit, he starts staying in shit. I didn't need that right now.

I promised myself two things I would never do when I left home. Never depend on a nigga and stay away from church boys. Fazio's money was long but I didn't need it, he never stepped inside of a church a day in his life, so I was winning.

"Can daddy get some of his chocolate pie, before he leaves?" Fazio asked in an exaggerated sexy tone as he gripped his hardened wood. I lost my virginity to Fazio last month, he was gentle with me and took his time. Eventually, I got the hang of it but it still hurt non the less. I made him use protection each time we had sex, he hated it but I didn't care.

"One time won't hurt, I need to feel the pussy." He would always plead, but I would never give in.

I continued to watch him play with himself, my yummy was already slippery, wet, and waiting for his mediocre dick. Fazio's dick wasn't huge like they talked about in hood books, but it was enough for my tiny tunnel.

"Come on bae, let me put it in raw." He begged as I got up and lifted my shirt. All I had underneath were boy shorts, so my plump ass was looking peachy perfect. I didn't have a huge ass, but it was enough and it was sitting pretty. No cellulite, no stretch marks, my body was right.

I took off my panties and was instantly welcomed by a gush of flowing juices, making its way down my legs. I was horny just as much as he was, but I wasn't having unprotected sex.

"Strap up baby and come taste this chocolate," I told him.

Fazio's face turned sour, but I didn't give a fuck. I was not being trapped with no baby, or a disease I couldn't get rid of. Until we were committed, I wasn't hearing it.

He walked over towards me with a different attitude. I could tell he was biting down on the inside of his lips, something he did often when he was upset.

"Turn around" He ordered as he grabbed my arm, his grip was tight and alarming. One thing Fazio never did was hit me, or call me out my name. Him acting this way kind of caught me off guard, since he knew from the jump I wasn't fucking raw.

I turned around doggy styled in the center of the bed, Fazio positioned himself behind me while holding on to my hair.

"I haven't met too many black girls with hair down their back, I can actually pull yours and wrap it around my hands a few times," Fazio mumbled as he bit the side of my face and pulled my hair forcefully, without notice he rammed his dick inside of me causing me to slip on my stomach. I laid flat out on the bed while Fazio drilled me from behind. I was spread-eagle, I was feeling pains in my stomach that reached my tonsils. I never had rough sex, so the pounding I was getting was brutal, but also satisfying.

"This pussy gonna be mine forever," he said while twisting his hips from side to side, digging deeper inside of me with every thrust. He finally got up and slowed down some, so I was able to get back on my knees and bounce my ass.

"Sister sister, I got my own mind." The music coming from my phone let me know Carlise was calling. I ignored it, but after the third time, I knew something had to be wrong. I reached over and grabbed my phone as Fazio continued to beat it up from the back.

Before I could say "hello," she was already screaming hysterically into the phone.

"Stop yelling Lease, what's going on?" I asked.

"Daddy found out." She cried.

I knew exactly what she was talking about, but I couldn't get any words out as Fazio's speed picked up. His pumps were intensifying, causing me to pump back harder. I put Carlise on mute because I was close to climaxing.

"Awe shit, what the fuck! This shit feels good as fuck." Fazio was louder than I ever heard him, the pleasure in his voice made me tighten my muscles around his meat as I played with my pussy lips. He grabbed my right titty and played with my nipple. Fazio continued pumping in and out of me while pulling my hair roughly.

"I'm cuming." He yelped.

Then it all made sense, once I felt his warm semen shoot off inside of me. This nigga done took the condom off and my sister could finally come out of the closet.

CHAPTER 6
Changes

Since the day Fazio released his unwanted seeds inside of me, I've been paranoid. I had a visit with my OBGYN next week, I called the morning after the incident and requested an emergency appointment.

"Why are you overreacting Bae, it was only one time?" Fazio said as he grabbed a black duffle bag from under my bed.

"That's not the fucking point, all it takes is one time and you should have respected my body as I asked you. Instead, you took advantage of me when I was in a vulnerable situation. I don't know where you stick your dick, we're not in a relationship, so what was the point, Faz?" I asked him with much attitude.

"The point is this. Yo ass is mine. I'm pretty sure yo' fine ass is knocked up since I'm the first nigga to nut in you. When you find out you're pregnant, I'll be right here to hold you. We may not be together, but for the next eighteen years we will be."

I looked at Fazio in disbelief, all this time he just wanted to trap my ass. The man that I was growing feelings for, was not the same person standing in front of me. I wonder if all the days and nights we spent wrapped in each other's arms was all a front or the times he told me he loved me. I fell for Fazio fast and hard, because he was my first.

"Listen here Carlonna Eloris Henderson, you're something special and if you think I'm going to let that go you're crazy. Yes, I have plenty of other bitches, but I want you. Have you ever heard that old saying, "If you can't have her, trap her?" Fazio mustard up a hearty laugh as he picked up his duffle bag and started to leave.

"Have you ever heard of ABORTION?" I shouted at his back as he made his way towards the door.

"If you ever try to kill anything that has my blood pumping through it, I'll kill you." He said seriously before slamming the door behind him.

With the toxic behavior that he just demonstrated something told me to run, but I did the exact opposite. Fazio was starting to change, but it turned me on for some odd reason.

Soon as Fazio left Carlise was at my door.

"Hey, sis!" Carlise said excitedly from outside of my room door. I put on a fake smile and greeted her, I didn't want her stressing about me when she had her own problems to worry about. Our dad kicked her out when he walked in on her and Ghani kissing, she's been here ever since.

"You good? You look a little down, is something wrong?" She asked while making her way towards my bed. The look on her face told me she wasn't taking my silence for an answer and I knew I had to tell her, it wasn't like I had anyone else to talk to.

I ended up telling her everything that happened between Fazio and me, even the part when we were fucking when she called me the night she was kicked out.

"Girl, you know what they say about the power of pussy, do you see how male dogs act when female dogs go in heat? Girl you done gave him some fresh shit too, be careful sis." Carlise looked at me seriously, before hugging me.

"Anyhow, the hell with me, what are you walking around cheesing for?" I asked her as I noticed how she looked overly happy, and if she kept it inside any longer she might explode.

"Well since you insist." Carlise paused momentarily before reaching inside of her bookbag, then she handed me a piece of paper.

"I've got accepted to travel with my forensic class, we will be leaving next month," she explained.

I was happy for her, even though I'd be alone I had to accept that my sister was graduating. She was becoming herself and her goal was to become a forensic anthropologist. I continued to read the letter, and it amazed me how she was selected from over three thousand students. Due to her grades, attendance, and her knowledge of the subject overall, she was chosen at number five. That was a big fucking deal!

"Wow, I'm so proud of you Carlise, this is amazing." I grabbed her and hugged her as tears slipped from my eyes. I didn't realize I was crying until my nose started running a little.

"You're such a big baby," Carlise said playfully.

"One more thing," she said as she stood in front of me.

"What's up?"

"Ghani was also accepted." Oh, that's great, I said dryly. I didn't want to come off as being jealous, but I didn't want to lose my sister. I wasn't trying to be selfish either, I just felt they spent so much time together already. I even allowed Ghani to stay over some nights, so that they could spend time with each other. They both were already going through a lot in this judgmental ass world. Once I started getting to know Ghani a little better, I was able to understand her more.

My phone started ringing letting me know my dad was calling, he didn't call much so I didn't know what would possess him to call now. Carlise rolled her eyes and started to leave the room, she stopped in her tracks when we heard our dad yelling through the phone.

"Get to Cook County emergency room now, it's your mother."

CHAPTER 7
Broken Heart

*a*s soon as we parked at the hospital, I jumped out and ran inside. Carlise was right behind me. Our dad spotted us before we made it inside, he ran over and hugged me.

"What in the world is she doing here." He said while pointing to Carlise.

"I'm here because the woman who raised me better than you ever could is here, this is not about you Carlon," Carlise spoke for herself.

"What happened to mom, is she alright?" I said cutting off what was going to be an unnecessary argument.

"She is in surgery, with lots of hope and prayers she should pull through," he said defeatedly.

"What the hell do you mean she should, what happened to her?" I was now yelling, I didn't know what was going on with my mom, he wasn't telling me what I needed to know and that was pissing me off.

"Your mother had a heart attack, she must have lost her balance and fell down the stairs."

Carlise held me like a premature baby as I fell to the floor, she dropped down with me in the middle of the emergency room and cradled me in her arms. All I could do was cry, I cried so much my chest started to hurt.

"Come on honey get off the floor, come sit on the chair." My dad said as he attempted to reach down and help me up, I immediately slapped his hand away.

"This is all your fault." I scolded him as Carlise helped me to my feet.

Hours passed by before a doctor came out into the waiting room, everyone sat attentively hoping it was their loved one's name that was called.

"The family of Mrs. Elora Henderson?" The young slim doctor, with sky blue eyes, called out. The three of us got up and made our way over to him, my heart was pounding at a rate I never felt before.

"Mrs. Henderson is requesting her two daughters," the doctor said as he looked at the three of us in confusion.

Carlise and I looked at each other, before looking at our dad. His eyes were saddened and the look of rejection crossed his face. I wasn't going to give him any sympathy until I found out what happened to my mom and Carlise sure was not going to show any compassion, we left him standing there and went to see our mother.

"Do you want me to give you some private time?" Carlise questioned as we walked the long hall.

"Girl you heard that man, she wants to see her two daughters, now let's go." I assured her while putting extra emphasis on *"Daughters."* I knew I was my mom's only biological child, but the love she had in her heart for Carlise was undeniable. I would never get in the way of that. I grew up a lot and being jealous of my sister was no longer my character. Since she was nine my mother has been in her life, that's eight long years of raising someone else's child, those years were the years when she needed a mother the most. The changes she went through with her body once she became a teenager, my mom was there for all of that. I knew how important it was to have a mom around during that time, we were only a year apart. Whatever I went through she was right behind me going through it. My mother was our backbone, there was no way in hell we could have gone to our dad about those personal things. I needed her, we needed her.

I stopped from reminiscing and once we got to our mother's unit, we were immediately stopped by a different doctor.

"I apologize, Mrs. Henderson was just rushed to emergency surgery, the first surgery caused a blockage in her arteries." Carlise and I just stood still, everything around me just seemed to spin way too fast. I felt myself losing my balance before a pair of soft hands grabbed me by my hand.

"Here, sit down right there." A medium-sized built, light skin guy said while guiding me towards a chair. His eyes are what had me mesmerized, they were green and almond-shaped. More like the color of an emerald stone, he had a light fade with waves neatly spinnin' around his head. He was gorgeous. I looked over at Carlise, who sat in a chair beside me. She was in awe just as much as I was and she didn't even like men.

"Just take a deep breath and relax, you'll get through whatever it is, and if you need a hand just give me a call." The guy said while handing me a card. He walked off and I examined the card he gave me. His name was Arico Martinez, he was some kind of youth director at a local church. I rolled my eyes in disappointment and threw the card in the wastebasket beside me, Carlise just looked at me like I'd lost my mind.

Our mother is back there dying from a broken heart, due to the actions of a church nigga. I'll pass on that fine ass devil. I thought to myself.

CHAPTER 8
You're Mine

*C*arlise refused to have a graduation party, she felt we had too much going on to celebrate. I didn't blame her, but I refused to allow her to sit around all day like she didn't just finish high school. I know with my mom still being in the hospital, and our dad disowning her had a lot to do with her mood. But I had it all under control.

We got a phone call early this morning, letting us know my mom was out of the woods. The hemorrhaging stopped and she was off oxygen, now we had to wait to see if she'd gain mobility. Carlise and I went to see her every day. My mom was a strong woman, so I knew she would pull through. I had to take Carlise's mind off of all of this, so I did something I never thought I'd do; I called Ghani.

Ghani agreed to put everything into motion, all I had to do was pay for a few things. Ghani's father was the owner of club DISCO, so she was able to rent it out for the night with no problem. Since she was graduating high school, the age limit was 16-23. Security was to be enforced and identification was required, we were going to make this a night to remember for Carlise.

"Why do you want me to put on that dramatic ass dress? It's not a damn wedding and I'm sure as hell not getting married," Carlise fussed. She was not the dress type of chick, but tonight she didn't have a choice. Ghani and I got this dress custom made and it wasn't cheap.

"Stop being a brat and just do what your sister asked." Carlise was surprised when Ghani spoke up and walked into her room. They both embraced in a long passionate kiss before Ghani shyly looked over at me.

"Don't be embarrassed now, you already sucked her damn tongue out, while I'm standing right here," I said. Carlise and Ghani just chuckled, while holding hands. I knew they hadn't seen each other in a few weeks, so I went out my way to make the whole day special. Ghani was preparing to leave, her mother was sending for her. Ghani was part Korean, she'd be staying in South Korea for college. I knew Ghani was scheduled to leave next month, and I wanted them to spend as much time together as possible. I left them both in Carlise's room and went downstairs, I still had a few things to get in order for the party tonight. Hopefully, Carlise wouldn't put up a fight about wearing the dress, since Ghani was here.

My phone continued to buzz from calls and messages, it was almost celebration time and I wasn't even at the club yet. I continued to ignore the calls because I was already running behind. Fazio had already sent me about ten messages asking where I was, he wasn't my nigga so I didn't answer him. I hurriedly finished my makeup, before admiring myself in the bathroom mirror. I strengthened my hair to the T, it reached to the middle of my back. My dark black hair was beautiful and the blonde highlights I added went perfect with my dark skin. I wore a Chinese bang to hide my big forehead and even added the highlights to the bang as well. Even though today was an all-white affair, I didn't want to outdo Carlise since it was her day. I decided to wear a less dramatic white dress that hugged my body and made my perky C cups look ravishingly delicious. A slit went all the way up my right leg, stopping right above my knee. My small, rump behind wasn't the least bit noticeable in this dress, but my beautiful face made up for what my body lacked. I glued on some long eyelashes and plucked my eyebrows. Once I was complete, I twirled in the mirror, like a high school girl, awaiting the arrival of her prom date. I was looking flawless and I knew it.

The night was filled with love and laughter, Carlise was astonished when she walked into the club. We partied hard with everyone in attendance, the love was real and everyone who showed up brought a gift.

I made my way to the dance floor with Carlise and Ghani, I started grinding on some sexy chocolate boy, who was only an inch taller than me. I was five foot four and hated short guys, but tonight I just wanted to have a good time, so I didn't care.

"It looks like you're having yourself a good time." A familiar voice said from behind me. I already knew it was Fazio, so I turned around to face him.

"Damn "O" I didn't know she was yours, I would have never disrespected you." The boy I was dancing with said, with a look of fear covering his entire face.

I looked between the two and was instantly confused. Fazio had a look of death written across his face, so I broke the silence.

"First of all, I'm not anybody's. Secondly, it's my sister's graduation party and I'm enjoying myself." I told them. You could tell Fazio was annoyed, but I ignored him and started back dancing, but the dude I was dancing with was nowhere to be found.

"Looks like I'm your dance partner," Fazio mumbled devilishly.

I was still upset with Fazio and even though my pregnancy test came back negative a few weeks ago, I couldn't trust his ass. I left him on the dance floor and headed to the bar, I wasn't a drinker but I damn sure needed a drink.

As soon as I sat down, I was swarmed by men trying to buy me a drink. A guy who looked to be around my dad's age came to sit next to me, offering to buy me drinks and more. Of course, I declined, but he was persistent.

"Why are you even at a kids party you fucking pervert, find your way up out of here," Fazio ordered.

For some reason, he always found a way to interfere with my business like I couldn't handle myself.

"Listen here, if the lady wants me to leave her alone, she has a mouth, young blood." The older man said while still focusing his attention on me. If he would have been paying attention, he would have seen Fazio's right hook coming, but unfortunately, it was too late. Fazio was all over him like a mother bear, protecting her cubs. Before I could stand up, about five more guys came over and started stomping the old man out. As soon as the bouncers came over, I knew Fazio would probably go to jail. To my surprise the bouncers picked the old man up from the floor and tossed him out front, he landed awkwardly on the sidewalk as he winced in pain. Everyone inside the club wasn't fazed by any of this as they continued to party.

"Get your shit, you're going home," Fazio looked at me with a deadly stare like he wanted me to say something. Instead of arguing and causing more drama, I grabbed my belongings and left with him. I sent Carlise a message, letting her know I'd see her later on tonight. I didn't want her worried about me, God knows how long Fazio would try to keep me hostage.

We got into Fazio's midnight black BMW, the leather seat was warm and welcoming. I reclined my chair back just a little, I hated sitting up too straight in the front seat it gave me anxiety.

"You letting niggas hit my pussy huh?" Fazio finally spoke as I sat mesmerized in his passenger seat.

"Your pussy?"

"Yeah my pussy Lonna, so please don't play with me. I better be the only nigga between those thighs."

I just looked at Fazio and shook my head, this nigga had some nerve trying to tell me what to do with my body. Even though I wasn't fucking nobody, he didn't need to know that, I wasn't his fucking property.

"You know what, lift that dress and slide them panties to the side," Fazio said before pulling to the side of the road. I knew he was crazy, but not this damn crazy.

As soon as the car stopped, Fazio already had two fingers inside of me. After a few minutes, he pulled his fingers out and smelled them, like I was some kind of scratch and sniff. Afterward, he inserted both fingers into his mouth and licked them. He looked at me momentarily before smiling.

"Still smell fresh and just as tight as the first time I beat them walls up, good girl." I just smiled at Fazio because he did something to me, his hardcore bad boy attitude turned me on. Even though I wasn't ready for commitment, Fazio knew he'd always have a special place in my heart. I guess this was the feeling you get when you lose your virginity to someone. Fazio and I shared a long deep kiss before we were startled by lights flashing behind us.

"Awe shit," Fazio said while looking through the rearview mirror.

"Listen, Lonna, you're mine, and don't forget that shit. I don't give a fuck how long I'm down, I'm coming back for you no matter what." That was the last thing he said before we pulled off, leading the cops on a high-speed chase. I sat in the seat not knowing why this was happening, when I looked in the backseat everything started to make sense. There were about eight black duffle bags back there, anyone in their right mind already knew what that meant.

"Get out and run," Fazio said as he pulled over on a side street, the sirens were close by so I did as I was told.

"Please just let me help you," I offered.

"I said go Lonna and remember what I told you." Fazio slammed the passenger side door shut and pulled off. About five cop cars flew past me, so I took off running. I was no fucking Bonnie, so Clyde was on his own.

CHAPTER 9
Dope Boys Do It Better

I couldn't believe Fazio had me out here running like a stray dog, I was pissed. Not only did I have on stilettos, but this dress was way too tight and I couldn't breathe. I was in an unfamiliar area, with a dead phone. My heart started racing as I came across a group of men standing on the corner, rolling dice, and smoking weed.

"Hey y'all, let the lady through." A guy who looked around my age said as everyone stopped what they were doing, and focused on me.

"That's Faz lady, one of y'all take her home while I watch the block. Shit is hot out here tonight, she doesn't need to be out here." A different dude spoke up. I just looked at each of them, there were about 15 of them standing around me. Without notice, the guy who just finished talking walked over to me and put his sweater around me. He smelled like expensive cologne, and he looked like he stepped out of a GQ magazine. He was fine as hell, with a swag that screamed DOPE boy. Tattoos were scattered all over his body, giving him a bad boy persona.

"Thank you, but I don't no y'all niggas. How do I know y'all not trying to kidnap my ass or something." I asked while looking at the one who just put his sweater around me.

"Girl ain't nobody finna kidnap yo' boujee ass, Fazio already called us and warned us to be on the lookout for you. Now if you don't mind we have shit to handle, so get in the car so I can take you home," he said while making his way to an all-white Bentley. At that moment I saw dollar signs, it was obvious that Fazio was involved in some illegal shit. I wondered what he did that he needed to run from the police, but then again it wasn't my business. I reluctantly got into the passenger side of this unknown man's car and prayed that I made it home safe.

Once I was inside his car, he introduced himself.

"Listen ma, My name is Kane. You are Fazio's girl so that makes you one of us. You don't have shit to worry about, we gone make sure you're good out here. Fazio gave us orders to protect you with our life, and that's what I intend to do. I already know where you live and where your family lives, so don't be tryna disappear in shit because Faz ain't having that."

I sat comfortably in Kane's leather, heated passenger seat, listening to him ramble on about a nigga that I wasn't even official with. Fazio wanted to control me, but I wasn't having any of that shit. I don't do bids, because soon as niggas get out of jail they go right back to all the bullshit they were into before they went into the pen. I've heard about couples who were together for years end up single because niggas don't appreciate a good woman. I refused to hold a nigga down, just for him to come home and shit on me.

I wasn't too familiar with the trap lifestyle, but I wasn't ignorant of it either. Even though I had a special place for Fazio in my heart, I wasn't going to put my life on hold for someone who only wanted me because I was fresh meat. I never went anywhere with him and he never offered, so what did we have besides sex in common? Nothing! I thought.

I looked over at Kane who was focused on the road, his brown skin looked so smooth. The only imperfection he had was a cut under his right eye, but the scar made him even more appealing. He had big juicy lips, that would probably suffocate my pussy. His hair looked freshly cut and did I mention the boy could dress his ass off.

"Yo, if you need anything make sure you holla at me," he said as he licked his lips. He pulled in front of my house and I just looked at him as his long tongue circled those perfect lips, an unknown sensation made its way from my pussy to my heart. I never felt that shit before. When you only had one sex partner all your life, I guess you never really know what to expect.

"You can get out now, ma," Kane said while looking at me. I laughed out of embarrassment and got out of the car. Kane got out of the driver seat and made his way to my side, once I got out he walked me towards my house.

Kane and I chatted for a few minutes before he slid me his digits, then he hopped back in his car and pulled off. I'm not too sure if he felt the chemistry that I felt, or if his loyalty to Fazio was more important. I didn't know what I was doing, but I knew that being with one man for the rest of my life, just to get hurt like my mom, was not my plan.

I sat on my front steps and took in the fresh air, summer nights were always refreshing.

"Hey, I remember you. Are you doing better?" A familiar voice made me jump, which only aggravated me. I hate being scared.

"Oh yeah, I remember you too. The church boy who saved me from busting my ass at the hospital."

"I guess you can say it like that. Do church boys bother you?" He stared at me, waiting for my answer. I just chuckled lightly before I got up off my stairs.

"I don't do church boys, I heard dope boys do it better," I told him before walking up the remaining stairs. I walked into my home and shut the door behind me. His fine ass did something to me, but it could never happen.

Once I got inside, my living room was filled with boxes. I was confused until I saw Carlise and Ghani coming downstairs.

"I'm glad you made it home safe, I heard shit got real for you," Carlise said while placing a box on the floor.

I shook my head in agreement, so she would take the hint that I didn't want to elaborate at this present moment. Instead, I changed the subject.

"Why are you packing, what's going on?" I asked, looking back and forth between the two of them.

"Well since your phone is going straight to voicemail, I'm assuming you haven't heard so I will fill you in," Carlise said as she stopped messing around with the boxes, and focused her attention on me. She then continued.

"Mom is ready to come home in a few days, she has gained activity in all of her limbs and is fully functioning on her own."

I jumped up and down like a little kid in a candy store, as tears poured from my eyes. Carlise and I embraced momentarily before I took a few steps back from her.

"What does that have to do with you packing?" I asked.

Carlise looked over at Ghani like she wanted her to speak up. I looked at Carlise seriously, waiting for her to respond.

"You have done so much for me Carlise, it's my time to grow up and make my own decisions. Tomorrow Ghani's mom will be sending for us, I will be on the first plane to Korea in the morning."

"Are you fucking serious right now Lease, your willing to throw away everything you worked for, over her?" I was pissed off, and she knew it. Ghani looked at me with sadness written across her face, but fuck her, she was taking my sister from me. Carlise wasn't moving around the corner, or up the street, she was moving to a whole different country.

I left them both standing in our foyer. I made my way upstairs to my room with mixed emotions, my mom was coming home and my sister was leaving home.

CHAPTER 10
Sleeping With A Boss

"**Mom**, please come stay with me. It's more than enough room in this house for both of us, and then some." I have been trying to persuade my mother to come to live with me since Carlise moved out two months ago, I was lonely. Kane made it his business to stop by almost every day, but that wasn't enough for me. My mom was now one hundred percent better, and I needed her to stay that way. Rumors were going around that my dad was bringing one of the missionaries from the church into their home when my mom was in the hospital. He wasn't shit, so I didn't put it past him.

My mom made a million and one excuses as to why she was staying. I didn't understand how a near-death experience did not wake her up, she went right back to my dad's toxic ass. He was a wolf in sheep's clothing, and it was a shame my mom was too blind to see it.

Since I couldn't get her to come to stay with me, I made it my business to check on her every day. We ended our call and she assured me she was fine, but I knew better. Instead of dwelling on shit that was out of my control, I hopped in the shower and got dressed. My sister was gone, I didn't have any friends, and I had nowhere to go. I decided to get real cute and go for a stroll.

About ten minutes into my walk, a car that I was too familiar with pulled beside me.

"Why do you think it's okay to walk around with your ass hanging out? I know you got more class than that," Kane said as a cloud of smoke escaped his passenger side window.

"Boy gone, you ain't nothing but somebody's bitch. You take orders, now you trying to give them because your boss is gone." I rolled my eyes and continued to walk.

"Listen ma, don't get fucked up, get in the damn car." I stopped walking and looked at Kane, he had a look on his face that would have killed me instantly. I didn't know him too well, but I could tell he was more savage than Fazio. Just from being around him the last few months, I knew he wasn't one to be played with. Kane opened the passenger side door from the inside, and I got in.

"Here, try some of this." Kane handed me a blunt, I never smoked but I knew what it was. I didn't object, I took the blunt and inhaled. Before I knew it, I was coughing uncontrollably.

"What the fuck did you give me? that shit almost killed me," I said in between coughs.

"You got virgin lungs, ma. You'll be alright. I wonder what else is virgin about you?" Kane was turning me on in a good way, I could feel the wetness already building up between my legs. I didn't answer his question though, I would probably say the wrong thing anyhow. I was still an amateur, and he looked like he had too much experience for my liking.

We drove around the city for hours as Kane handled different transactions. My lungs were growing accustomed to the weed since all Kane did was smoke. We passed blunts back and forth the entire time, I couldn't keep my head up, I was too damn high.

"I'm grabbing a room for the night, getcha shit and let's go, he said as he pulled into a fancy hotel. I looked at Kane, then back to the hotel.

"What if Fazio finds out?"

"Listen ma, Faz about to do some big time. I wanted you first anyhow, but he beat me to it. Now if you gone hold the nigga down for life, find your own way back home, but if you gone be mine, let's fuckin go," Kane said in a way that made me bubble inside. The weed already had me feeling myself, so I got out of the car and followed his lead.

Kane already had the room set up, it was a bit romantic and I didn't expect this kind of treatment from him. I wouldn't think dope boys had a romantic side, but I was mistaken.

Kane ordered us a nice dinner, along with a bottle of Moet. After dinner, I was told to follow the rose petals. The rose petals led to a bathroom with a huge champagne glass filled with water and bubbles, it had stairs leading to the top. It was beautiful.

"Let me explore your body in the king-sized water bed, ma. I promise to be gentle," Kane said while reaching for my hands. I reluctantly grabbed his arm and got out of the champagne glass. He looked so muscular and solid with his shirt off. I got shook when I looked down at his wet shorts, and his dick print was visible. There would be no way all that was fitting inside of me, he was way out of my league.

"I said I got you ma, now come on." Kane said, noticing the change in my demeanor.

Kane led me to another door, once he opened it I damn near had a heart attack. I was still a complete novice when it came to sex, so to see all the sex toys that laid across the bed kind of freaked me out.

Kane looked over at me and smiled, he could sense how opposed I was. Once he finally got me in the room, we laid down and smoked a nice fat blunt. Whatever kind of weed we were smoking, sure eased any worries I had.

"Let me take the lead, you just relax with ya fine ass." Kane dried both of our bodies off and then told me to lay on the bed. I laid on my back, and he immediately opened my legs. My little kitty was already waxed, so I happily showed her off. My kitty had very low mileage and was well kept, I knew Kane would go crazy when he finally explored her.

"Damn ma, yo pussy lookin' phat down there, I can't wait to taste it," Kane said as he licked those big juicy lips of his. Inside I was scared as fuck, I have never seen a dick this big before. Fazio didn't have half the package he had, and that had me second-guessing myself.

Kane surprised me when he poured oil all over my body, from my baby toe up to my collar bone. I was drenched in oil, but I was relaxed and I felt good. After he finished massaging the front of my body down, he flipped me onto my stomach. Starting from my shoulder blades, he made his way all the way down to my ankles. It wasn't until he made his way back up, that I felt his stiffness touch my ass. His hands circled my round ass, and he slid his index finger inside of my wetness. I tensed up a bit, but immediately relaxed when he began planting kisses all over my back. Kane grabbed a toy from beside me, he turned a switch and a miniature bullet started vibrating.

"Get on yo back, ma. I'm about to take you to another level." I bit down on my bottom lip and did as I was told.

"Oh my, What the fuck is that!" I shouted out as my body jerked, and my legs started shaking.

I knew what a bullet was, but I had no experience with it. I saw one in Carlise's drawer one day, and she gave me the details. I washed my hands five days straight with bleach after touching her toy, I refused to touch one again. But tonight I could understand why she and Ghani used it. My body trembled and I grabbed hold of the sheets, the bullet was vibrating on my clit and Kane was sucking my pussy lips, causing me to lose the little bit of control I had left. My body started to go stiff as Kane slurped all of my juices up, my chest heaved up and down uncontrollably.

"It's more from where that came from, but for now I'm just giving you the samplier. I can tell your damn near a virgin and Faz is more than likely the only nigga you fucked, so I'm gone work with you and then I'm gone wife you."

I just sat there looking dumbfounded, his handsome ass just turned down some fresh pussy.

Kane walked over to me and kissed my forehead. He grabbed a briefcase from the drawer beside me and opened it.

"I'm gone be out taking care of some things, I know you don't fuck with nobody so I think you should spend some time with your mom. Go get her out of the house and take her somewhere," he said as he threw two stacks of bills on the bed and left the room.

I laid back in bed and smiled, Fazio never did no shit like this before. I now realize I was settling for less being with Fazio. None of that mattered though, I was sleeping with a boss now.

CHAPTER 11
Fast Lane

*L*ife was moving fast for me, sometimes it was moving a little too fast and I was having a hard time catching up. Being with Kane for over a year now has been the best thing that has happened to me, he is my soulmate and he brought out the best in me. He showed me things and took me places I have never seen, he made me feel like I was his number one girl and I was loving it. Whenever business called he kept me away from it, even when I volunteered my services he would refuse. He called me his queen and made me feel above any bitch, if any hoe had a problem he was putting them in their place. Sex with him was unexplainable, his dick was huge but he made me feel comfortable. It was never just sex with him, he would always explore my body and do things I never experienced before. Kane showed me he loved me, and since my mom wasn't going to move in with me, I moved into his condo with him. Since that day, our bond grew and everybody knew I belonged to him.

"That will be $257.25," the cashier said as she popped her gum, snapping me out of my thoughts and reminding me I was in line. I paid for my items and headed out of the mall. My phone started ringing, letting me know Carlise was calling. She was an entire day ahead of the US, but she made it her business to check in on me every day. I chatted with her on the phone while putting my bags inside my car, I was a licensed driver now and I was always on the go. Kane bought me a pink Bentley for my 20th birthday and I was loving it.

"I still feel bad I missed your birthday party, I know Kane did it big for you," was the last thing I heard Carlise say before a plastic bag was placed over my head. I dropped the phone immediately and tried to fight back. I was suffocating myself even more trying to swing, but I wasn't going down without a fight. I heard a few female voices around me, so I knew they had to be some jealous ass haters since I didn't have problems with anyone. I knew if they got me on the ground they would beat me bloody and fuck up my cute face, so I fought my hardest to stand.

"Y'all bitches done really fucked up," was the next thing I heard before someone grabbed me. I started swinging on them too, I couldn't see shit with the bag still over my face. After a few minutes of wrestling, the bag was finally snatched off my head. I scratched at my throat and gasped for air.

Kane grabbed me and held me in his muscular arms, I was shaking like a fucking leaf. I looked around the parking lot and saw four bitches laid out. I started to charge them, but Kane scooped me right up and put me into his car.

"Y'all niggas know what to do with them hoes, make them wish they never touched my queen and bring wifey car back to the crib," I heard Kane say to his men before he got in the car. My ears were ringing from getting punched in the head and I could feel my eye swelling, those bitches did a number on me.

"You won't have to worry about another bitch getting that close to you again, I promise you. I'll paint this whole fucking city bloody red and burn Chi-town the fuck down before somebody ever touches you again," Kane said seriously.

"You know who they are don't you? It was probably some bitches you fucking behind my back, why else would four bitches sneak me and try to kill my ass?"

Kane inhaled hard before speaking, his face was distorted and his veins buldged out the side of his head. "I do know them bitches and like I said they will get dealt with," he left it at that and pulled off. I could tell he was boiling inside and from his reputation, I knew the four of them bitches would be floating in Skokie River by midnight.

Once we made it home, Kane got a hot bath ready for me. My body was sore but my dark skin didn't bruise easily. That was one plus about being chocolate. After my warm, relaxing bath, Kane picked me up and placed me on the bed, he dried my body with a towel and then oiled me down. He picked me out some pajamas and helped me get dressed.

"I'll be back in a few hours, get some sleep," he said while planting a kiss on my busted lip. Before leaving he grabbed me a bucket of ice and a fresh towel for my face, it would help with the swelling on my left eye.

After he left I called my mom, my phone was cracked just a little but it worked. I gave her all the details from the events of today, and she was kind of quiet. I knew something was wrong with her if she wasn't talking since she could keep you on the phone for hours.

"Mom, why are you so quiet?"

"I'm fine honey, I was just listening to you and your drama-filled lifestyle," she said slyly.

"You got some nerves mom, don't judge me when you're getting cheated on by a man of God. That's why you're so bitter now."

"Chile please, being bitter is not in me. If I was bitter, your sister and brother would have never stayed in this house, this house would be burned to ashes if I was bitter. So no babygirl, I'm not bitter, I'm *broken*. I allowed it and now I'm the only one who can fix it. My broken pieces are for me to put back together and when I'm ready, I will. But don't you ever confuse my brokenness with bitterness, because I'm a strong ass black woman, and don't ever forget that shit."

I apologized to my mom before we hung up, I knew she been through a lot and I never meant to sound disrespectful. I think I was upset because she wasn't listening to me and I needed someone to listen without judging. I didn't know why she felt some kind of way about being called bitter, but I knew it struck a nerve.

After talking to my mom, I called Carlise. She was freaking out because I hadn't called her back, and she was on the phone when I was attacked. She even went so far as to call our dad, something she never does. We ended up talking for over an hour and I could tell she was enjoying life. Everything about her sounded different, she was free. She was over there living the good life, and I was over here living the hood life. I would have never imagined I'd be caught up in this lifestyle, I was living in the fast lane and the traffic was fucking crazy.

CHAPTER 12
Reap What You Sow

W alking with Kane along the lakeshore, with my perfectly manicured feet gripping the sand was so relaxing. Yesterday was his twenty-second birthday and when I told him I never been to Navy Pier, he told me my "Black Card " was revoked.

"I still can't believe your saditty ass ain't never been to the pier, Fazio was keeping you on house arrest or something?" He said while holding my hand. I just smiled at him as we continued to swing our interlocked hands back and forth. The last person on my mind was Fazio. Kane bought me a new phone and got me a new number since Fazio couldn't stop harassing me. When he found out Kane and I was a thing, he promised he would get out and get me back. The man couldn't take no for an answer and Kane was ready for war. I didn't want any drama or gunfight at my expense, that's not something I was fond of. I loved Kane and no one could replace him, but niggas always had a point to prove.

"Whatcha thinkin' bout, ma?" he asked while kissing my hand. We have been together for almost three years, and every time his juicy lips touched me I still got chills.

"I'm just enjoying the moment with you baby, that's all." Kane didn't need to know that I was worried, I knew how Fazio got down and I didn't want anything to happen to him. Kane could hold his own for sure, but it shouldn't have to come to all of that.

We ended our night at the Pier on speed boats, we probably rode the Ferris wheel about ten times. Billy Goat Tavern happened to be my favorite food spot, but nothing beat The Botanical Garden; it was stunning. This life was what I wanted for my mom, and it was sad because we didn't have to travel far to see things we never saw. My mom didn't have any freedom, but once she got a taste of it I knew she wouldn't think twice about leaving my dad.

A loud commotion a few feet in front of us, immediately grabbed Kane's attention as his trusted men jogged over towards us.

"We got problems boss, you and wifey need to get out of here quickly," Kango told him while trying to hurry us along. Kango was Kane's first cousin, they grew up like brothers and they resembled each other as such. Kango was a big dude though and he was nothing to play with, I saw him in action and it wasn't a pretty sight.

"What's going…."

"Pop! Pop!"

Kane's words were cut off as bullets flew aimlessly. Kango and a few others returned fire, but they were outnumbered and outgunned.

"Get her the fuck out of here now!" Kane shouted.

"I'm not going anywhere without you," I screamed as tears filled my eyes. I hated how

Kane always wanted me out of harm's way, but he would put himself in the way without hesitation. Kane reached in his waistband and pulled out his pistol.

"Give me one, I know how to use it," I told him as he kneeled behind a food cart next to me.

"Listen, baby, this ain't the fuckin movies and you ain't Angelina Jolie, so sit cha pretty ass right here and let me take care of these pussy ass niggas," Kane whispered.

A bullet made its way into the cart we were hiding behind and luckily for us, it missed us.

"We gotta move from this spot, a few of my men are down and I don't have no one to get you outta here." Kane said calmly.

"Ah fuck!" Kango yelled as his body hit the ground a few seconds later.

Kane jumped up and let off three rounds as he made his way over to Kango. I watched as he helped move him from out in the open. Kango was hit and in a lot of pain. A man in a mask was approaching both Kane and Kango, and neither one of them were aware. I tried to make different noises, but I couldn't get Kane's attention. I grabbed a ketchup bottle from the food cart and tried my best to aim at the masked man's head. Once I shot the bottle, the unknown man pointed his gun directly at me and I froze.

"You thinking about killing my queen, well think again pussy," Kane said as he squeezed the trigger and let off two shots into the side of the man head. The gunfire started to ease up as more of Kane's men arrived.

Kane's best friend KC rushed over to me and placed a coat over me, before picking me up and carrying me to an all-black armor truck. Kane was right behind us shouting out orders to his street soldiers, making sure they handled everything properly. KC opened the door to the truck and I climbed in, I held the door open for Kane, but he was no longer behind me. I scanned the area to see where he went that fast. A few minutes passed before I saw Kane running and shooting at the same time.

"Go fuckin help him," I yelled at KC from the back seat. My door was locked from the outside, I couldn't get out if I wanted to.

Kane ran and jumped into the passenger seat, before KC could pull off bullets ricocheted off the truck. Just as we were pulling off, the police were pulling up.

"What the fuck is up KC? Call them and tell them niggas to get Kango to the hospital now." Kane fussed from the passenger seat as he was making calls of his own.

"Pull up to the main trap now and have a driver take wifey home," Kane yelled into the phone before he hung up abruptly.

Once we pulled in front of Kane's trap house his army was already ready, cars piled the street and about thirty people stood around with guns in plain sight. Kane got me situated inside and set the alarms, six of his ruthless young boys stayed back with me and stood guard outside of the house.

My phone started singing Boyz II Men "A Song For Mama," so I knew my mom was calling.

"Your dad was just rushed to the emergency room, I think he had a stroke," my mom said hysterically into the phone. I took a deep breath and tried to feel some kind of remorse. He was still my father and I loved him dearly, but there is an old saying, "you reap what you sow," and Carlon Henderson sowed many bad seeds.

CHAPTER 13
Not Bitter

*M*y mom stood in the hall talking to the doctor, while I sat in a chair next to my dad. He was alert and ready to go, but they weren't ready to release him just yet. Four days ago he suffered a mini-stroke, he was lucky my mom responded as quickly as she did or he wouldn't have made it. His blood pressure was way too high and he had a kidney infection.

"See what happens when your old ass thinks your still a spring chicken, running around fucking these young girls done gave your ass a stroke. Your old ass need to sit down somewhere," My mother said seriously while walking back into the room, a look of disgust written over her face as the veins in her forehead tightened.

"See what happens when you're an old bitter bitch!" Retorted my dad.

I looked back and forth at them while they argued like toddlers, that last comment must have bothered my mom. She walked slowly towards him clenching her fist, that's how I knew she was upset.

"Your black ass is lucky I put up with you all these years. I don't see how these young hoes can deal with your little, wrinkled shriveled up dick. I stayed so long because I saw potential in your weak ass, but just like you were out there doing you, so was I. The thing is, I'm discrete about my shit. Bitter means that I'm angry and that's something I refuse to be, you could never have that kind of power over me. I'm broken like a scattered jigsaw puzzle because of you, but I won't have to piece myself back together alone. Ask Pastor Martinez," my mother said matter factly as she knocked all of his food off the tray onto the floor, and left the room.

My mom's revelation shocked the hell out of me and from the look on my dad's face, he wasn't too happy. I didn't know who Pastor Martinez was, but if looks could kill he would be burying my mom. Little Carlon walked in the room, just as I was about to say my goodbyes to our dad. Little Carlon was back with his mother now, but he was such a daddy's boy. My dad always wanted a son and if the situation would have been different, I would have been happy for him. Little Carlon and I shared a quick hug before I left out of the room to find my mother.

As I walked down the hall my phone started to vibrate, the caller ID was unknown. I usually didn't answer blocked calls but something told me to answer.

"Who's this?" I whispered.

"Ya man said he will always come back for you, no matter what," an unknown raspy voice said, before hanging up.

My heart felt like it dropped down in my ovaries and a sharp pain shot through my chest. I stood there trying to remain calm so that I could call Kane, but my hands were trembling. My mom came from behind me and wrapped her arms around me, she grabbed the phone out of my hand and called Kane. After back to back calls and no answer, I knew something was wrong. I reached out to KC and a few others, but no one answered. I left the hospital to find my man, if it was me who wasn't answering, he would have been shut the town the fuck down.

I drove by Kane's main trap spot in Fuller Park, the entire house was surrounded by police, fire trucks, and paramedics. I jumped out of my car and made my way to the house, a cop stopped me right by Kane's car. A body laid on the ground, covered with a white sheet as bloodstains soaked through it. I looked down at the sneakers on the body and lost it, whatever happed after that had me waking up in the hospital four days later.

When I finally woke up, I wish I hadn't. KC told me Kane was gone and I missed his home going yesterday. He was shot five times and they cremated him. My heart was gone, my baby left me and didn't say goodbye. Something inside of me broke that day. If this is what my mom meant when she said she was broken, I didn't want to feel that shit ever again.

After losing Kane I fell into a deep depression. I stayed in the house we shared and smelled his clothes, wore his hats, and sprayed his cologne. When a deed to the house was mailed to me last week, it had me listed as the owner. I cried for days straight, it wasn't until Carlise flew in that I finally came out of the house. Since they were on Winter break, Ghani's mom paid for an emergency flight and Carlise stayed with me for two months. It felt good having my sister back around, we even paid a visit to our dad who was now in the nursing home. Carlise finally let the hurt go that he caused, she was happy and she needed him to know she forgave him. We didn't know how much time he had, he was diagnosed with brain cancer a few months ago and he took a turn for the worse. My mom was doing her own thing, she and Pastor Martinez was finally official. I still didn't meet him yet, but he had my mom smiling, her entire glow was different and she was truly free.

After spending a few months with the family, having little Carlon come over, and helping me out of my depression, it was time for Carlise to depart.

"Can you grab my bag out the hallway?" Carlise screamed from outside as the cab driver impatiently waited for her to load her belongings in the car.

I ran back into the house and grabbed her bag, I gave it to her and hugged her before she got in the cab. I waited for the cab to disappear down the road before making my way back inside.

Before I made it to the first step, I smashed right into someone. My phone dropped out of my hand and I tripped over a rock trying to avoid stepping on my phone. A pair of smooth, strong hands grabbed me, making me feel warm and fuzzy inside. His cologne was light but noticeable.

"This wouldn't be my first time saving you, I think it's fate, what do you think?" A familiar voice said. I looked up at him and immediately forgot how handsome this green-eyed devil was.

CHAPTER 14

Church Boys Do It Better

Who would have thought I would be dating a church boy? Not Carlonna Henderson. Well, Arico and I are officially a couple. The day he wrapped me in his arms and broke my fall for the second time, was the day my life changed for the better. I gave Arico the run around for months until finally, I gave him a chance.

That was two years ago, and I no longer call him the green-eyed devil, he was so much more than that.

"Good morning beautiful, are you ready to meet up with your mom and my dad?" Arico said as a smile spread across his face and he planted a soft kiss on my forehead.

The world was so small that the pastor my mom was dating, was Arico's father. The day at the hospital when she said Pastor Martinez didn't phase me since I wasn't into Arico back then. Arico took me to his church one day and I was surprised to see my mom there. Once they found out Arico and I were dating, they ended their relationship. They have been best friends for over four years now and have a mutual understanding. I refused to have a stepbrother who was also my boyfriend, that was not normal.

I checked myself in our full-length mirror in the hall, making sure my clothes weren't too tight fitted. Church folks did not play about that and the mothers of the church weren't going for it. I've been attending New Hope Ministries for a year now. I saw a man of God in Arico's father, something I didn't see in my own father. My dad passed away last year and in that same year, I decided to give the church a try again.

I ran my fingers through my hair, my curls bounced down my back as I shook my head back and forth. Years of going natural and properly taking care of my hair had my hair at a length I never thought it would reach. I had inches!

I made my way downstairs in a black ankle-length skirt, a red blouse, and red pumps. Arico waited for me at the bottom of the stairs, he held his hand out for me once I reached the last step. He looked so handsome in his all-black suit, tempting to say the least. Arico and I have never had sex, that's what made our relationship so special. He had several failed relationships and wanted to save himself for marriage, I knew that when we got together and I respected his decision. The way he treated me was already satisfying my appetite, sex would just be a bonus.

Arico set the alarm to our home and we left out. His security measures were a little dramatic, being that we stayed in an upscale area in Buffalo Grove. The area was surrounded by hills and the closest convenience store was about five miles up the road. It was a blessing Doordash was available out here, or I would have probably died of starvation when we would go low on groceries.

We met our parents at the church, my mother was looking fabulous. She was looking thickener since the last time I saw her, she even had a new companion. When she and Arico's dad stopped dating, she started talking to Deacon Myles. I heard of keeping it all in the family, but I never heard of keeping it all in the church. But, if she was happy, I was happy for her.

After church service Arico and I had a dinner date at a local barbecue joint, the food was fresh and delicious. Once our date ended we went and sat by the water, something that always made me think of Kane. I was truthful about my past, so Arico was already aware of my previous relationships. It was him who helped me get past Kane and find myself again, for that he would always have my heart.

"You shine different under the stars, you're so perfect," Arico said as he looked over at me. He moved in closer and we shared a deep kiss, his tongue entwined around mine while he played with my hardened nipple. I had the urge to pull out his shaft right there in public, but I knew better. I could see his dick imprint growing, he stood to his feet quickly to get his man under control. I couldn't help but laugh, he always got embarrassed when that happened.

"I'm going to marry you, Lonna, sooner than you know."

"You better hurry up, I'm not too sure how much longer your man can hold on," I told him while pointing down below.

We shared a few more hours by the water, before heading back home. It was days like this that made me sit back and reevaluate my life. I was lucky to be here, I was involved in things I shouldn't have been and witnessed things I never should have seen. Running from my mother's and father's demons, caused me to run into the hands of men who shouldn't have touched me. After Fazio, I should have left those dope boys alone. Even though Kane was my heartbeat, his lifestyle was dangerous. He left me for the streets, he loved those streets more than he could ever love me. I was happy, living a peaceful life with my man. I didn't have to worry about being shot riding in his passenger seat, or getting a phone call telling me he was killed in a drive-by shooting. I didn't know what all the hype was about dope boys, but church boys do it better.

EPILOGUE
Surprise Surprise

"**A**re you sure you want to cut your hair, girl?" Francine asked while holding a pair of scissors. I was at the hair salon and I wanted to try something different, cutting my hair seemed to be the obvious thing to do. I wanted Arico to see me switch it up. He had a dinner going on tonight at the house for my twenty-fifth birthday, I was hoping a different look would catch him off guard. My hair was now past my ass, chopping it down some wouldn't hurt.

"Yeah, I'm sure," I said unenthusiastically.

Francine didn't waste any time, she started clipping away. I knew some hairstylists get scissor happy, but Francine was an old friend of Kane's so I trusted her.

Once my hair was cut, trimmed, washed, straightened, and blew out, I was able to see it. Francine did her thing on my hair, she had me looking like a snack. I never got my hair done, so this had me feeling myself. Francine took off about 5 inches, my hair rested at the center of my back now. My jet black hair looked healthy as it shined exquisitely from the deep condition, and the hot oil treatment. I gave Francine a hefty tip before I left to go next door. I had a nail appointment right after.

Since I never went to any salons, I didn't realize how time-consuming beauty was. I spent half the day getting pampered at Arico's expense, and I was loving it. Arico being the cheif was the plan for tonights dinner, God knows what else he had planned for me, he always made me feel on top of the world. I didn't get finished with everything until after five in the evening, Arico was calling for the tenth time.

"Lonna baby, what is taking so long? I knew I should have gone with you." He fussed into the phone.

"This was all your idea Ri, you can't rush perfection baby."

"You're already perfect, now get home before the food gets cold."

As soon as I hung up with Arico, I made my way to my car. My nails were a little long, so I knew it would take me some time to adjust to them. I grabbed my keys out of my purse and hit the alarm to unlock my car. An all-black sports car pulled beside me, whoever was inside just sat there. I hurriedly got into my car, as it was impossible to see inside the darkly tinted windows.

Once I pulled out of the parking spot, the car beeped at me several times. I turned up the radio and made my way home.

I pulled into our driveway within a half-hour, Arico's car was the only one out front. The house looked dark from the outside, I didn't understand why he was rushing me if no one was here yet. My mom's car wasn't parked in my spot, so I knew she hadn't arrived yet. Men were so impatient for no reason, I thought to myself as I parked inside the garage.

"Honey I'm home!" I playfully shouted as I made my way inside the house. The kitchen was connected to the garage, so I grabbed a soda out of the fridge before making my way to the living room.

"SURPRISE!"

I dropped the can of soda that I held and clutched my chest, the screams startled the hell out of me as I tried to catch my breath.

"Oh my God, y'all scared me," I said as tears crept down my cheeks. I was crying happy tears, the sight in front of me was priceless. Carlise and Little Carlon were standing next to my mom. My aunts and uncles were there, my cousins and even grandma Elane came. After a few moments of everyone showing me love and taking pictures, Ghani walked out with a three-tier cake, it was beautiful. The cake was all white with huge Red roses on it, the number 25 sat at the top of the cake. Little Carlon turned the lights off and lit the candles, everyone started to sing happy birthday.

"Close your eyes and make a wish," my mom instructed. I closed my eyes and made a wish, once the lights came back on I started crying my eyes out. Arico was on one knee in front of me, holding a huge diamond wedding ring.

"Will you…….." Arico's words drifted off as a loud knock rattled the door.

"Knock Knock!"

The heavy knocks at the front door, caused everyone to shift their attention away from the proposal.

"I'll grab it, everyone just relax," I told the guest as everyone looked confused. Everyone I could think of was here already, so who was the late attendee disturbing a special moment. I thought to myself while making my way to the front. I opened the front door swiftly, I was a little aggravated at whoever was interfering with my engagement.

"SURPRISE!" A familiar voice said once I opened the door.

On God, I felt like I pissed on myself. I stood there completely frozen in shock, my head started spinning like I was back on the

Ferris wheel. My hands grew sweaty and my body's temperature felt like it turned up to the max. The last thing I remembered hearing was, "I told you I'd be back...No matter what." That's when everything went pitch black, and I could have sworn I felt my soul leave my body.

ABOUT THE AUTHOR

*A*ngelina Wilson is a 32 year-old, self-published author of eight novels. She was born and raised in Niagara Falls, NY. Her Memoir "This Life I Lived" is a best seller. She is currently working on more releases. She found writing as a way to escape reality at the young age of nine. Her mother would collect all of her poems, and any other writing material she wrote. It wasn't until the age of twenty-nine that she released her first novella, "Jailhouse Wifey."

In her spare time she also runs a non-profit organization, called "Speak Up and Live." Her passion is to help people, and that's one of the many reasons she is the founder of this organization.

You can find Angelina's books on Amazon. She can also be followed on Facebook and Instagram.

ALSO BY THE AUTHOR

Jailhouse Wifey 1 & 2(Completed Series)

This Life I Lived

Heavenly Revenge

Facebook Obsession

BLACK

His Secret Freak(eBook Only)

www.ingramcontent.com/pod-product-compliance
Lightning Source LLC
Chambersburg PA
CBHW070754120626
46557CB00002B/596